BLACKBERRY FARM

MRS NIBBLE

Jane Pilgrim

This edition first published in the United Kingdom in 2000 by
Brockhampton Press
20 Bloomsbury Street
London WC1B 3QA
a member of the Caxton Publishing Group

Designed and Produced for Brockhampton Press by
Open Door Limited
80 High Street, Colsterworth, Lincolnshire, NG33 5JA

Illustrator: F. Stocks May
Colour separation: GA Graphics Stamford

Title: BLACKBERRY FARM, Mrs Nibble
ISBN: 1-84186-041-7

Printed in Singapore by Star Standard Industries Pte. Ltd.

MRS NIBBLE

Jane Pilgrim

Illustrated by F. Stocks May

BROCKHAMPTON PRESS

Mrs Nibble lived with her three babies, Rosy, Posy and Christopher, in a little house in the bank of the field behind Blackberry Farm. Mr Nibble lived there too, when he had time. But he was a very busy rabbit, and did a lot of work in the burrows on the other side of the village. Mrs Nibble was a very busy rabbit, too, because with three children to look after there was always a lot of washing and cooking to be done.

But Rosy, Posy and Christopher
were very good little bunnies, and
played in the grass outside their
house while Mrs Nibble was doing
the work.

And in the afternoons she put
them in the pram, and pushed them
down to the village to do the
shopping. And in the evenings, when
they were all tucked up in bed, she
did the ironing and the mending.

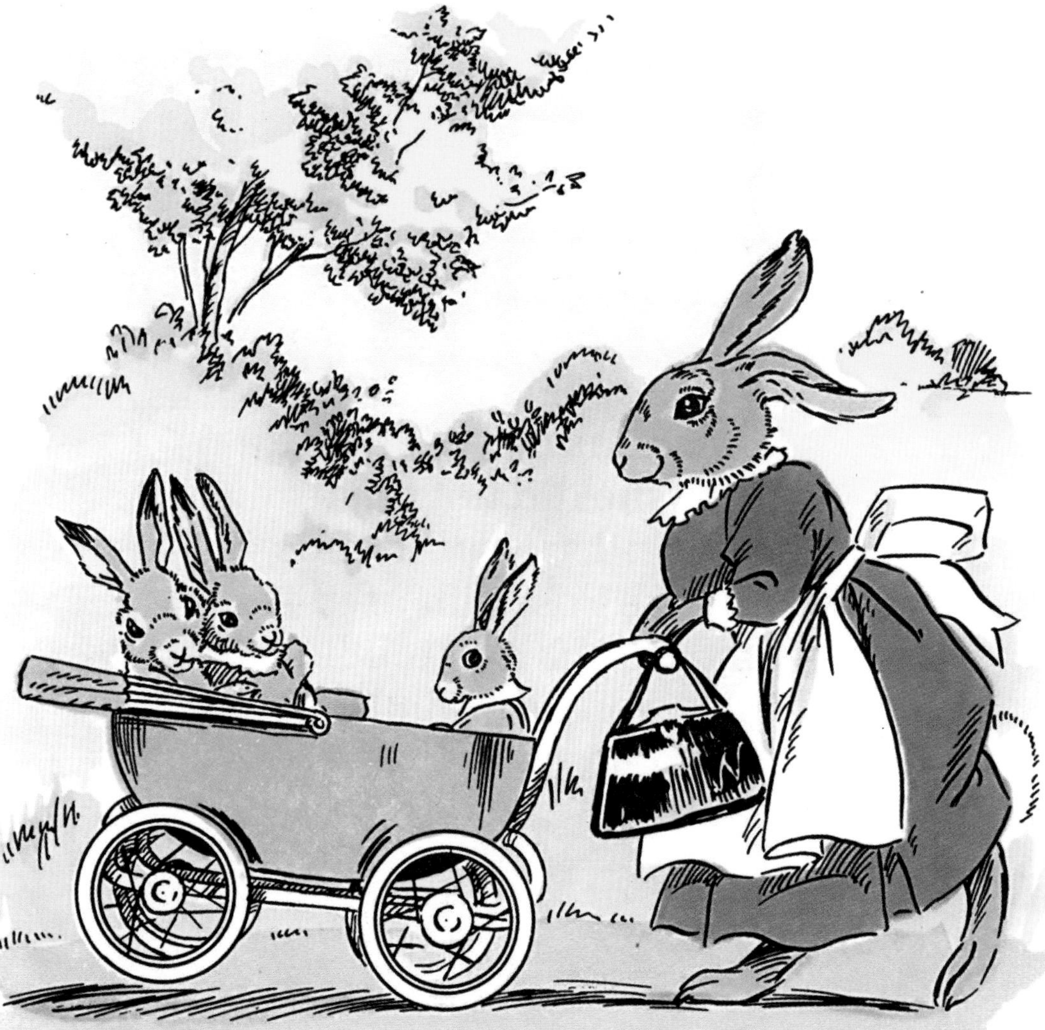

Mrs Nibble was a very friendly
rabbit, but she did not have much
time to go and see her friends –
so Joe Robin the Postman used
to fly round most days and tell
her all the news when he brought
the letters.

One day Joe flew round in great haste after breakfast, and told Mrs Nibble that a lot of the little bunnies on the other side of the village were ill in bed. "I've heard they are covered with spots," he said, "and are sneezing something terrible."

Mrs Nibble was most alarmed. "It's quite true," Mr Nibble said at lunch-time. "Ernest Owl thinks it's the measles. He should know, because he's wise." So they watched the little bunnies very carefully. But Rosy, Posy and Christopher did not have any spots, and they did not sneeze, and they ate up their meals beautifully. So Mrs Nibble forgot all about the measles, and began to work hard – planting out lettuces and thinning the carrots.

And then one day at tea Rosy sneezed five times. "Bless you," Mrs Nibble said, and lent her a handkerchief. And then Posy sneezed five times, too. "Bless you," said Mrs Nibble, and fetched another handkerchief. And then Christopher sneezed – and Mrs Nibble wiped his nose for him, because he was the youngest.

But when Mr Nibble came in to his tea, they all sneezed together – seven times each, without stopping. Suddenly Mrs Nibble remembered the measles in the burrows on the other side of the village. She flung up her paws in horror, and looked across the table at Mr Nibble. And he nodded his head gloomily at her.

MRS NIBBLE

Without a word Mrs Nibble
cleared the tea-table, and got the
bath ready in front of the kitchen
fire for Rosy, Posy and
Christopher. She undressed them,
and put them all in the bath, and
then she looked at each one.

There could be no doubt. They were all covered with spots. Quickly she washed them, and dried them, and tucked them up in their little beds, and gave them each a mug of warm milk and a bran biscuit, and kissed them good night.

In the morning Ernest Owl came and looked at Rosy, Posy and Christopher. He saw their spots, and heard them sneeze and took their temperature. "You must keep them in bed," he told Mrs Nibble, "until all their spots and sneezes have gone. Give them plenty to drink, and keep them warm. I will come again in a week's time."

So Mrs Nibble kept Rosy, Posy
and Christopher in bed for a week,
and Mr Nibble brought them some
new toys to play with. And Emily
the Goat was very kind and gave
Mrs Nibble some extra milk when
she heard the children were ill.

When Ernest Owl saw them a week later, he was very pleased with them, and told Mrs Nibble they could get up. "I am starting a school at Blackberry Farm soon," he told Mrs Nibble. "You must let Rosy, Posy and Christopher come. Just lessons in the morning. I will let you know when term begins."

Mr and Mrs Nibble were very
pleased when they heard about the
school, and in the evenings, while
Mr Nibble read aloud to her, Mrs
Nibble sat beside the fire in the
little house in the bank of the
field behind Blackberry Farm,
making new clothes for Rosy, Posy
and Christopher for their first
term at school.